P9-DMA-373

AUDREY WOOD

Illustrated by
DON WOOD

THE
NAPPING
HOUSE

RED WAGON BOOKS
HARCOURT BRACE & COMPANY
San Diego   New York   London

Text copyright © 1984 by Audrey Wood
Illustrations copyright © 1984 by Don Wood

All rights reserved. No part of this publication may be
reproduced or transmitted in any form or by any
means, electronic or mechanical, including photocopy,
recording, or any information storage and retrieval
system, without permission in writing from the
publisher.

Requests for permission to make copies of
any part of the work should be mailed to:
Permissions Department,
Harcourt Brace & Company,
6277 Sea Harbor Drive,
Orlando, Florida 32887-6777.

First Red Wagon Books edition 1996

Red Wagon Books is a registered trademark
of Harcourt Brace & Company.

Library of Congress Cataloging-in-Publication Data
Wood, Audrey.
The napping house.
Summary: In this cumulative tale, a wakeful
flea atop a number of sleeping creatures
causes a commotion, with just one bite.
[1. Sleep—Fiction. 2. Fleas—Fiction]
I. Wood, Don, 1945– ill. II. Title.
PZ7.W846Na   1984 [E] 83-13035
ISBN 0-15-256708-9
ISBN 0-15-256711-9 (oversized pbk.)
ISBN 0-15-201062-9 (miniature edition)

The original paintings were done in oil
on pressed board.
The text type is Clearface Roman.
The display type is Clearface Bold.
Separations were made by Heinz Weber, Inc.,
Los Angeles, California.
Printed and bound by Tien Wah Press,
Singapore

F E D C B
Printed in Singapore

For Maegerine Thompson Brewer

There is a house,
a napping house,
where everyone is sleeping.

And in that house
there is a bed,
a cozy bed
in a napping house,
where everyone is sleeping.

And on that bed
there is a granny,
a snoring granny
on a cozy bed
in a napping house,
where everyone is sleeping.

And on that granny
there is a child,
a dreaming child
on a snoring granny
on a cozy bed
in a napping house,
where everyone is sleeping.

And on that child
there is a dog,
a dozing dog
on a dreaming child
on a snoring granny
on a cozy bed
in a napping house,
where everyone is sleeping.

And on that dog
there is a cat,
a snoozing cat
on a dozing dog
on a dreaming child
on a snoring granny
on a cozy bed
in a napping house,
where everyone is sleeping.

And on that cat
there is a mouse,
a slumbering mouse
on a snoozing cat
on a dozing dog
on a dreaming child
on a snoring granny
on a cozy bed
in a napping house,
where everyone is sleeping.

And on that mouse
there is a flea. . . .

Can it be?
A wakeful flea
on a slumbering mouse
on a snoozing cat
on a dozing dog
on a dreaming child
on a snoring granny
on a cozy bed
in a napping house,
where everyone is sleeping.

A wakeful flea
who bites the mouse,

who scares the cat,

who claws the dog,

who thumps the child,

who bumps the granny,

who breaks the bed,

in the napping house,
where no one now
is sleeping.

in the napping house,
where no one now
is sleeping.